LEABH

D0264890

The Savage

## Other books by David Almond

# the SAVAGE

## David Almond

### Illustrated by

## Dave McKean

WALKER
BOOKS

LEABHARLANN

UIMHIR DL0650194

RANG

For Peter Mortimer

D. A.

For Liam,
who discovered
his inner savage

D. M.

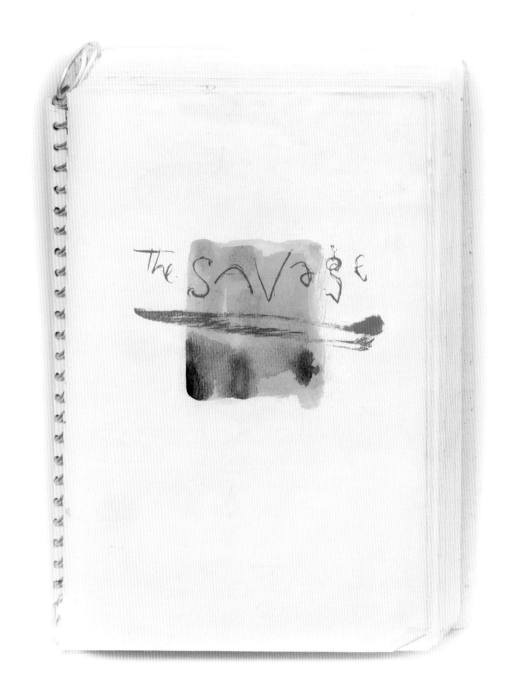

# ONE

You won't believe this but it's true. I wrote a story called "The Savage" about a savage kid that lived under the ruined chapel in Burgess Woods, and the kid came to life in the real world.

I wrote it soon after my dad died. There was a counsellor at school called Mrs Molloy, that kept taking me out of lessons and telling me to write my thoughts and feelings down. She said she wanted me to explore my grief, and "start to move forward". I did try for a while, but it just seemed stupid, and it even made me feel worse, so one day I ripped up all that stuff about myself, got an old notebook and started scribbling "The Savage". Here's the first bit of it, and I know the spelling isn't brilliant, but I was younger then.

There was a wild kid living in Burgess Woods,

I wrote.

He had no famly and he had no pals and he didn't know where he come from and he culdn't talk

and he lived on beries and roots
and rabbits and stuff like old
pies that he pinched from the
bins at the back of Greenacres
Rest Home. He lived in a cave
under the rooined chapel. His
wepons were old kitchen nives
and forks and an ax that he
nicked from Franky Finnigin's
alotment.

If anybody ever seen him he chased them and cort them and killed them and ate them and chucked their bones down an aynshent pit shaft.

He was savage.
He was truely wild.

11

Once I started writing the story, it was like I couldn't stop, which was strange for me. I'd never been one for stories. I couldn't stand all that stuff about wizards and fairies and "once upon a time" and "they all lived happily ever after". That's not what life's like. Me, I wanted blood and guts and adventures, so that's what I wrote. I set it all in our little town of Saltwell. I didn't show "The Savage" to Mrs Molloy. I didn't show it to anybody. It was my kind of story, just for myself.

# TWO

My name's Blue Baker by the way. I live down Aidan's Lane at the edge of town with my mam and my little sister Jess. We're OK now. But we weren't back then. We'd been an ordinary happy family, not a care in the world, then without any warning everything changed. One day Dad was there with the rest of us. The next his heart stopped, and he wasn't. I won't go into all the stuff about the funeral and everything because it was just a b***** nightmare. And I won't try to say how we all felt, because no matter what the Mrs Molloys of the world say, there's no way you can get your feelings properly down on paper. I'll just say it was all absolutely b***** horrible. And I'm sorry about the swearing, but if you can't swear about something like this, what's the use of swearing at all?

Anyway, Mam said it was worst for me. She said she'd had my dad for a dozen years and more, so she had lots of happy memories. And Jess was that young she'd never really remember him. But me, I'd always remember and wonder what I'd missed, and I'd always feel the loss of never getting to know him properly. "Lads need their dads to grow up properly," she said. I knew it was true, but I tried to be strong. I said as soon as I could I'd go out and get a job and look after us all. She laughed and said, "Will you now? What kind of job?"

I didn't have a clue, of course.

"One that'll get me loads of dosh," I said. "I'll be a pop singer." And I started yelling out a pop song. "Or a footballer," I said, and I dribbled a ball of paper through the kitchen. I rolled my sleeves up and started shadow-boxing in the living-room. "Or a boxer." I showed how big the muscles on my arms were getting (not very big at all) and Jess giggled and Mam felt them and admired them, then she cuddled me.

"Just be a lad, son," she said. "That's all you need to be for now."

And we held each other tight.

Right from the start, I tried not to cry. I tried to put on a real tough front. The thing is, I've never really been one of the hard lads. I know how to swagger about when I need to, like most lads do, but like most of us I'm just dead soft inside. But there are some proper hard lads out there, and they're the ones to keep away from. Lads like Hopper.

Hopper. What can I say about him? What is it about some kids? Why do they want to make life so rough for other kids? Whatever it is, Hopper was one of them. He was bigger than me, a couple of years older. He lived not too far away from us. He had a home-made tattoo of a skull on his brow and "LOVE" and "HATE" tattooed onto his knuckles. He walked around smoking and sneering and spitting and swearing. He'd always picked on me, far back as I could remember. There was nothing special about that – he picked on loads of kids, 'specially the scrawny ones like me. And there was nothing really dangerous about it. He just called me names – Ratface, Dogbreath, stupid stuff like that. And he'd lurch into me when I walked past, and sometimes

15

DL0650194

spit out the side of his mouth at me. Like everybody else, I just tried to keep out of his way. I told Dad about it a couple of times. He said he wasn't surprised. He'd seen the way Hopper went about, and he knew the Hopper family from way back.

"I know it's hard, son," he said, "but there's always been kids like Hopper and there always will be. You just have to try and ignore them."

I flexed my muscles (they were even scrawnier then) and put my fists up and punched the air.

"Sometimes I wish I could smash his face in," I said. **"Kapow!"**

Dad put his hand up flat and we played at me thumping it, like we had done since I was little. I thumped and thumped, and tried to imagine that Dad's hand was Hopper's face. We laughed, and Dad pretended my thumps were really hurting, and he said, "I know it's awful, son. But what you've got to remember is that a bully like Hopper is just showing how weak he really is. And you know what? He's probably jealous, as well."

"Jealous?" I said.

"Aye, son, jealous. Because you're a happy lad from a happy home. And, sad to say, he's not." He shrugged. "I will have a word with him, but the best plan is just to ignore him. When he sees he's getting no response from you, he'll go away."

But just a few weeks later it was my dad that went away, and Hopper was still there, and when he saw how wounded I was, it was like he smelt blood and started moving in for the kill.

The day after the funeral I was going up to the Co-op for some bread when Hopper appeared and stood in my way.

**"Hey, Dogbreath,"** he said, and I could smell the stink of his smoky breath. "That dad of yours was at our door last week. Did you know that? He said you'd been whingeing on about me. So you know what I said to him?" He paused while he spat and took a drag on his cigarette. "I said, 'P*** off and die, Fatso.' And would you believe it, it's worked!" He laughed and flicked his cigarette butt out into the road. "That's what you get if you mess with Hopper."

He stepped aside and let me pass.

"Aaaah," he mocked. "Is skinny little Dogbreath blubbing?"

From that day on, I hated him with all my heart. But I couldn't bother Mam about it, not with what she was going through, so for the first time, there was nobody at home that I could tell.

I did tell a couple of mates, but they were lads like me – tough on the outside, soft at the heart. Joey Sullivan just shuddered and said he'd go nowhere near a pig like Hopper. Max Mack said I should go to the police. Louie Carr told me to make a wax model of Hopper and stick needles into it at midnight.

And I told Mrs Molloy. She said much the same as Dad did: try to ignore it, try to understand that it shows how inadequate Hopper is. The way she went on about it, though, it was like she was as concerned about Hopper as she was about me. She told me to write it down, of course, along with all the other stuff, and I did try to do that, but surprise surprise it was no b***** help at all. Nothing seemed to be any help. Then I got on to writing "The Savage", and just a few pages in, Hopper started to make an appearance.

Here's the bit where the savage sees Hopper for the first time.

# THREE

It was a brite and suny morning in Burgess Woods.

The savage was sittin on the stones that hid the entrans to his cave. He had been owt hunting in the nite and he had a chiken on his nee. He was ripping it up and biting bits off it and blud was trikling down over his chin. He was drinking a bottel of Fanta that heed pinched from the back of The Grey Horse. It was a delishus brekfast. There wos birds singing all arownd and the sky was clear and the savage was realy happy.

20

Sudenly there was a moovment near by.

He crowched down and licked the blud from his hands ...

and gript his nife and watched.

There was a kid coming thrugh the trees. He had blak raggy jeans on and a pare of blak Nike traners and his hare was all messy and he was dead ugly. The savage didn't no it but the kid was calld Hopper and he was horribel. Hopper tryd to scare people and he made life horibel for nice kids, specially if they were weak or sad. The savage didn't no any of that but he could tell strate away that the kid was no good and he hated him strate away and he gript his nife tite.

Hopper was just wanderin with a stupid blank look on his face. He lit a cigaret.

The savage had never seen nothing
like it. Why was the kid puffin smoke
like he was burnin inside? What was
the point of that? So the savage new
the kid was stupid.

He wanted the kid to come closer, so he cud kill him and chuck him
down the pit shaft. (He didn't want to eat him tho, cos he looked like
he wud taste too horibil.) But the kid Hopper didn't come closer that
day, he just went on wanderin and lookin stupid.

As he went away, the savage crept after him. He watchd the kid gowing out of the woods, crossing the footbridge over Badger Brook, walking back towards the town. He watchd him dissappear from site and he ran his finger over the sharp blade of his nife. He stud where Hopper had stud and he smelt the smell of Hopper still lingerin in the air.

28

He wandered about for a minnit with a stupid luk on his face like Hopper did, and he stud for a minnit like Hopper stud, and he put his hand to his mouth like he had won of them smoky things and he breethed in and owt like Hopper did so he new how horribil it felt to feel like Hopper. Then he grunted and growled. He knew he would always remember the stupid ugly kid Hopper. And he knew he wud see him agen.

# FOUR

When I wrote all that, I felt much better. It was great to see Hopper through the savage's eyes, and to write how ugly and stupid and horrible he was. It was great to think that if there really was a savage in the world, he would help me to sort Hopper out.

I wrote loads, page after page of adventures, and it was brilliant. The savage was mainly active at night. He raided allotments and gardens. He broke into sheds and chicken coops. Sometimes kids were disturbed in their sleep and they looked out of their bedroom windows and saw a strange shadow moving through the night. Sometimes people coming back from late-night parties or lock-ins at The Grey Horse came across the savage, but nobody ever really believed what they had seen. They told themselves they were mistaken. They thought they were dreaming or drunk. How could there be a savage like that living in an ordinary sleepy little town like ours?

And of course if they came too near to him, or if they saw him too closely, it was the end for them. They'd be clubbed or knifed or axed, then dragged back to his woods, eaten, and flung down into the pitch-black pit shaft.

I did drawings of the savage as well. He was the same size as me but with bigger muscles and teeth like a wolf and feet as tough as a horse's hooves. He wore a dog skin round his waist and chicken feathers on his head. When I drew him and wrote about him, I could see him, I could hear him, I could smell him. Sometimes, it was nearly like I was him and he was me.

One day, without really thinking about it, I put myself in the story for the first time. I just found myself writing down that I was with Jess, holding her hand. It was a lovely summer's day. I had a little rucksack on my back. We were heading out of the town. We went down our lane and across the little footbridge over Badger Brook into the woods. Once I got going with it, I wanted this bit to be really special so I laid it on thick. When we got up to the chapel, we settled down on a patch of grass. I got some egg sandwiches and some biscuits and a bottle of pop out of the rucksack. The grass was green and soft and there were flowers all around us. The sun was shining down through the trees, there were a few fluffy clouds, and the flowers and the grass danced gently in the breeze.

I had Jess dancing and skipping and singing with the sun in her hair and butterflies fluttering round her head. I sat her down and started reading poems to her – stuff about daffodils and skylarks and sunlight. I wanted it to be like one of those scenes from a film – innocent and happy people frolicking about and relaxing in the sun, and all the time being watched by something dangerous and wild.

The savage crowched in the rooined chapel and watched. He had been hunting last nite but he had cort nothin but a littel mouse and a frog and he was hungry. Very hungry.

And the scrawny kid and the littel girl
looked tasty. He had Franky Finnigins' axe
in his hand. He got ready to jump out and
chop them up. He growld. The boy turnd and
looked and thort he saw somethin but
couldn't be shure, and the savage seen the
boy's eyes and he seen he wasn't a evil kid
like the last one that had been up here.

And he saw the littel girl was lovely and innosent and good. So he stayed still and he kept out of site and he watched, and soon the girl was dancing agen and the boy was lying there on the grass and starin into the sky like he was wondering about the anser to some grate grate mistery. And sumthin changed inside the savage that day. He started to see that there was diffrint kinds of people, and some was more good than bad, like these nice kids, and some was more bad than good, like the other ugly kid. So he left these two alone.

And the boy lookd towards him agen, and agen thowt there mite be somethin there but he couldn't be sertain. And the boy and his sister finishd there piknick and headed back down towards the town. The boy turnd back one last time from the footbridge at Badger Brook, and he seen somethin moving in the trees, some stranje-shaped being. And the boy waved, and he shouted,

My name is Blue! And this is me littel sister, Jess!

But there was just silens in reply.

The boy took hold of his sister's hand tight, and hurried home with her. Behind them the savage stood where they had stood and sat where they had sat, and he smelt there sent, and he danced like Jess had danced, and stared into the sky like it was a mistery and he gabbled a bit like he was saying poems, and it felt strange and diffrint to do those things. He still felt like the savage but like somethin else as well. And he growled softly and he jabered out loud like he was saying words, just like the boy had when he'd yelled their names.

**38**

But of cors the savage had no words,
just jabbers and grunts and gasps,
and he new nothing abowt words.
How cud he?

But he was starting to lurn.

# FIVE

One night I was deep in a dream and then Mam was shaking me and waking me up.

"Blue," she whispered. "Are you OK, Blue?"

She said she'd heard me grunting and grinding my teeth in my sleep. I couldn't speak at first, then I grunted that I was OK, it was just a dream.

"I was worried," she whispered.

I smiled. I rubbed my eyes. The moon was shining in on us through the bedroom window.

"I was in a cave in Burgess Woods," I muttered. "I was eating a rabbit."

She laughed, and I laughed too in a sleepy way. I didn't want to wake up properly. It all seemed so real. I still had the wild scent of the savage in my nostrils. I had to hold up my hands in the moonlight to check there was no blood on them. Mam stroked my head, and there seemed no point in not telling her.

"And I was with a savage," I said.

"A savage?"

"Aye. A savage. A savage from my story."

Her eyes widened. I reached under my bed and pulled my notebook out. I switched the little bedside light on and showed her the pages and pages of scrawl and the drawings of him – his weird clothes, his blood and scars, his wild hair, his huge muscles, the wild look in his eyes.

She shook her head in amazement.

"And what happens in the story?" she said, so I told her the basics of it and described some of his adventures.

"You're so clever, Blue!" She laughed. "I had no idea you had this in you!"

"Neither did I!" I said. "I just started and kept on going and going and going."

She pulled her dressing-gown closer and folded her arms.

"Would you read me a bit? Go on, son."

I shrugged and said OK, if she really wanted me to. I didn't want to read any of the stuff about Hopper or about me and Jess, and I didn't want to read anything too gory and bloodthirsty, so I found a bit I'd written a couple of days back, about the time the savage went to Stokoe's pig farm.

"Are you sitting comfortably?" I said.

"I am," said Mam, so I started.

The savage had been stuffin hisself all day with rabbits and burds and berrys and he was ful and his stomak was groanin and he needed some exersise. He got his ax and went owt in the moonlite and wandered thrugh the woods.

After a bit there wos a funny stink and he cud hear soft gruntin and snufflin. He followd the smell and the sound and he fownd hisself at a farm, and he didn't no it but it was Stokoe's pig farm.

Mam giggled and clapped her hands.

"Stokoe's pig farm!" she said. "But that's a real place! I've been there myself."

"Course it's a real place," I said. "But did you see a savage there?"

She giggled again.
"Go on!" she said.
"What's next?"

He climed over a fense and he
fownd loads of wooden pens with
pigs in them and a couple of them
grunted and woke up and come
owt of their pens in the moonlite
to look at this straynge savage in
their field.

And the savage lookd at them and new
they wud be very tasty but he wosnt
hungry, so he just grunted bak at them
and lookd bak into there shiny eyes.
And won of the pigs nuzzld him like he
wanted to be frends, tho of cors the
savage didn't no what a frend was.

**45**

And the savage got an idea and he got close to the pig and got up onto the pigs bak and the pig snortid in suprize. But it didn't seem to mind and it started walkin then trottin rownd the field then runnin.

And it grunted as it ran and the savage grunted to and wavd his ax
in the air and the ax shone in the moonlite. And a cuple of other
pigs joind in, runnin rownd and rownd the field with the pig with the
savage on its bak. And they were all havin a grate time. And in the
farmhows, the farmer Stokoe stirred, and his wife Mrs Stokoe did
too, and she sed wot on earths goin on out there, Stanley? And he
sed, I don't know, pet. And they got up, Mr Stokoe in his stripy
pijamas and Mrs Stokoe in her flowery nitie and lookd owt of the
window and cudnt believe there eyes. And the savage on the pigs
bak turnd and lookd at them and snarled and waved his ax at them,
then he jumpd down off the pig and went runnin off into the nite.
And Missus Stokoe lookd at
      Mr Stokoe and sed,

I think we                    and Mr Stokoe sed,
shud just go                       I think
bak to sleep,                    yore right,
   love,                            love.

So they lay bak down agen and went back to sleep
again cos they thort it must all be a dream.

I shut the notebook. Mam giggled again and clapped her hands.

"The Stokoes!" she said. "And their farm, and their smelly pigs, and the savage! It's fantastic. Where on earth…?"

Then she stopped, and we listened. Jess was crying.

# SIX

Mam brought Jess into my room. We sat there on my bed and the moon shone in. We cuddled her and tried to soothe her, but she was sobbing hard.

"Daddy," she gulped. "Want Daddy."

"Oh, love," said Mam. "Oh, my little love."

Then Mam forced her face into a smile and said, "Hey, you'll never guess what. Our Blue's writing a story for us, Jess. Aren't you, Blue? Go on. Show her the funny pictures."

So I showed Jess the pictures of the savage and I made a funny savage face and I did a funny savage grunt and Jess giggled through her tears. Then Mam told Jess about the smelly pigs, so I read that bit again and I trotted round the room like I was on a pig's back and I waved my hand like I had an axe in it. And it worked. She giggled and her tears dried. We all sat close together again and Jess slowly went to sleep.

Mam and I just looked at each other.

"I'll put her back," she said.

She kissed my brow.

"You're a brave and clever boy," she said. She winked. "And you're a savage, too."

And she switched off my bedside light and they left me.

I stared into the moon. I felt sad, small, frightened, furious, bitter, lost, lonely… But like I said, there's no words that can say how I really felt. I stared into the moon and stared into the moon. Then I switched the light on again, and I got my notebook and my pen and I started writing fast and hard.

# SEVEN

Yes the savage was startin to lern about words. Yes, the savage wos learnin abowt what it felt like to be human, and yes the savage was lernin abowt good and bad in people, but the savage wox still the savage, and sumtimes he was nothing but a savage — crewel and vishus and hard as b***** nails.

Sumtimes all he cud think of was butcherin and killin and
bein savage and wild. This nite he was sharpenin Franky
Finnigins nife on a rock and he was gruntin and growlin and
snufflin and suddenly the memry of the horibil kid
Hopper come into his mind. He rememberd how
ugly and stupid he was. He rememberd the
stupid smoky thing he put in his mouth.
He rememberd his horibil smell and
his horibil face and the horibil
memry of it made him wild.

And he new he had to find
Hopper and get rid of him.

So he left his cave and crawled
threw the rooined chapel and
headed out the woods and rite
into the town.

He walkd up Aidan's Lane. He sniffd as he walkd and he pawsed owtside Blue and Jess's howse cos he could smell there smell and there wos another nice smell there that he didn't no, but it was the smell of Blue and Jesses mother.

He smelt it for a wile then he went on thrugh the silent streets and lanes, past The Grey Horse and the post office and the Co-op and it wosn't long before he was standing at another gate and sniffin the air and this tyme it was the gate of Hopper's howse and the smell there was just b***** horibil.

He went threw the gate to the door and shuvd his nife blade between the door and its frame and he twisted and the door opend and he went inside sniffin all the time.

And the smell led him up the stairs and to the dore of Hopper's room. And he opend the dore and slipped inside.

It was stinkin and pitch black in there but the savage's eyes were brillient at seeing in the dark and strate away he seen Hopper lyin in his bed fast asleep.

He didn't hesitayt. He stood at the bedside. He rased the axe up high above his hed and...

And I couldn't
do it, not even
in a story. Like
I said, I'm not a
hard lad and now
I knew that the
savage wasn't either.
I'd been writing dead
fast. Now I hesitated.
The savage lowered
his axe. I sighed
and wrote on.

The savage couldn't do it. He'd been
dreamin of doing it all the way owt from
Burgess Woods, and now he couldn't do
it. He growld. He lowerd his axe. He
looked at horribil Hopper, then he
punched him hard in the face. That
punch woak him. The next one bust his
lip, and blood pored from his nose.

The savage pulled the curtain open so that Hopper could see him by the lite of the moon, so Hopper could see the mussels and the wild eyes and the dog skin and the chicken feathers and the ax, so he could see how savage and dangerous and wild he was. He lifted his fist again and glared down at Hopper, like he was daring him to try somethin, but Hopper cudn't move. He just stared in horror at the wild thing in his room, and he wimpered, "No! Don't! Please don't!"

And the savage growled and snarled and bared his teeth and spat rita in Hopper's face and he waved his fist like a last warnin, then he went back owt into the nite, and he stood out there in the street in the littel town and he danced like Jess had done in the woods that day and he waved his ax round his hed in triumf.

Then he walked agen, and paused agen outside Blue and Jess's house and he pressed hard against the door and it opened.

He climed the stairs in silens.

He opend Jesses door in silens. He stud over her, then he reached down and rested his hand on Jess's brow, and there was tears in his eyes.

He tried to speek like Blue and Jess had in the woods that day.

He tried to say poems, but all he could do was go,

Agh! Ugh! Agh!

like always, but the sownd was gentil, gentil, and like it was full of tenderness and care. He rested his hand on her brow agen, then he left the room, left the howse, and headed back towards his cave.

# EIGHT

Will you believe what happened next? You have to, because it did happen. Because it's true. When I woke up next morning I could hear Mam's voice coming from Jess's room. She was laughing gently. I got out of bed and went into Jess's room.

"What a mess," Mam was saying. "Can you not even keep yourself clean when you're asleep?"

She turned round as I came in.

"Just look at this lass," she said.

And when I looked where she was pointing, I saw the grubby mark on Jess's brow, and it was just like a hand print. Mam was rubbing it clean with a tissue and Jess was giggling.

"Look. Am scruffy, Blue!" she said, then she slipped back into baby-talk, copying Mam's murmurs of affection. "Ga. Goo. Ah." And when I heard that, I heard the savage's grunts, too.

"How did you get so dirty?" I said.

"Was playin in the mud!" she giggled.

And Mam wiped the mark away and we had breakfast together and inside myself I told myself, "No. No. It couldn't possibly be true," and Mam looked at me and said, "You OK, son?"

"Aye," I said.

She tousled my hair.

"You'll be thinking about that savage, eh?" She sipped her tea and smiled, remembering last night.

"Stanley Stokoe and his pigs!" she said.

Soon afterwards, I headed out for school. And I passed close by the Co-op where Hopper was. And he had a bust lip and a black eye and such a weird look that when I passed him he hardly even noticed me. Again I said to myself, "No, it couldn't be true." But I turned and went back to him.

"Hopper," I said, but he didn't hear. "Hopper!"

He stopped and looked at me. I went up to him.

"I know what happened," I said. And he tried to look hard and careless, but he couldn't do it. "I know about the savage in the night." He stood there with an axe, didn't he? He punched you, didn't he? Once, twice, and you were b***** terrified, weren't you?" Hopper just stared at me, like he'd stared at the savage last night, and it was brilliant. He started to turn away but I caught his arm and I went even closer. "I sent him, Hopper," I whispered. "I made him do what he did. Do you believe me?" He said nothing. It was obvious that he didn't know what to believe. "And I'll send him again if you don't lay off." And I grinned and left him there and walked to school without a backward glance and inside it was like I was dancing and waving an axe in triumph.

# NINE

That day was like I was living right inside the savage's story, like the savage was living right inside me. I couldn't concentrate in lessons. I pretended to listen, pretended to work, but I kept closing my eyes and straight away I was in Burgess Woods with him. I was beside a fire deep down in his cave. I was slurping water from a can and chewing roots and berries. In English it was easier, because we had to write stories, so I just got on with the savage's tale. I scribbled fast and free and the pages became like the story in my notebooks – scribbles and scrawl and doodles and drawings. And it maybe looked like a mess, but it was a mess that made sense, that made a story on the page and in my mind that was as vivid and real as the real world. Then I was aware of the teacher, Miss Brewer, standing at my side, looking down at me and my work, and I realized that I was grunting and growling as I wrote.

I felt her hand on my head, heard her ask, "Blue. Are you all right, Blue?"

And I looked up and all the class were staring at me.

"Would you like to speak to Mrs Molloy?" said Miss Brewer.

"No!" I grunted.

But she got her anyway, and Mrs Molloy crouched at my side and stroked my arm.

"Come along, Blue," she said. "Come and tell me what the trouble is. You know you can speak to me."

But I couldn't speak. I grunted at her. I grunted again.

"Oh, Blue," she said, trying to be tender.

And I couldn't stand it. I bared my teeth and snarled at her like the savage would and I grabbed my book and pen and jumped out of my seat and ran out of the room and headed for the woods, and all the way, on street corners and in lanes between houses, and as I entered the woods and went deeper into the woods, I kept stopping, scribbling the next bit of the story, and the next bit, till I was right there, walking towards the ruined chapel. And I was terrified, but at the same time somehow deadly deadly calm. I stood among the stones in the chapel and I wrote a few more words.

The savage herd a noise outside in the chapel, and he new that the boy Blue had come.

The savage growled softly. He waited in the dark.

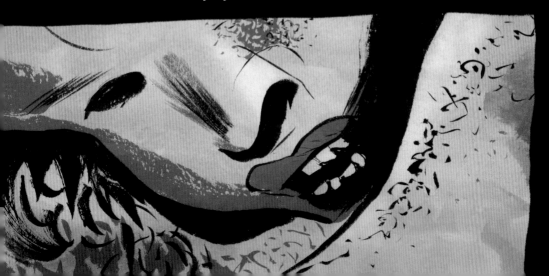

Owtside, the boy stopped writing. He crawld thrugh the stones towards the hidden cave beneath.

I stopped writing. I crawled through the stones towards the hidden cave beneath.

# TEN

I crawled through into the darkness. Soon I was clear of the stones and I crouched and stood up. The cave floor was soft and sandy. There was the flickering glow of a fire much further in. Nothing else to be seen. Then I caught his scent. I heard his breath. I saw his eyes, shining in the dark, and he growled. I trembled. I didn't run. I moved closer to him. I felt his hand on my arm, and I knew he'd been waiting for me, that ever since I'd started the story we'd been bound to meet. It was like we'd known each other always.

"My name's Blue," I said.

"Agh," he murmured. "Ugh."

He led me further into the cave, further towards the fire, and by the low light of it I saw him face-to-face like a reflection, and he was just like me, only weirder and wilder and closer to some magic and some darkness and some dreams.

He grunted and I grunted back at him.

"Agh! Ugh! Agh!"

I opened my book and showed him my drawings of him.

"This is you," I said. I showed him all the words. "And this is you, as well. Look. That says 'the savage'."

I ripped out one of the pages and gave it to him. I gave him my pen. He growled. He led me closer to the fire and we saw each other more clearly, and we cast our eyes across each other and stared into each other's eyes like we were staring into some great mystery. Then he leant down towards the flames and lifted a burning branch. He held it high, towards the wall of the cave and I almost tumbled when I saw what he had led me here to see.

It was me, there on the cave wall. I was drawn in charcoal and coloured with the dye from leaves and earth and berries. There I was, sitting, leaning over a desk, writing. There I was, lying on the earth and staring into the sky. There was Jess, dancing beneath the sun. There was Hopper, with his skull tattoo and his cigarette. There was Hopper, trembling in his bed. And there was the savage, dancing, waving his axe beneath the moon. I grunted, muttered. I had no words. The pictures on the cave wall were works of wonder.

"Agh," he whispered. "Ugh."

And he drew me further, beyond the fire, and he held the flames high again and he caught my arm and steadied me.

It was me, a little smaller, a little younger, and Jess as a baby, and Mam, and Dad. The four of us were there together, sitting at a table with smiles on our faces, so happy. The savage watched me as I stared, as I realized what it meant; as I realized that the savage had drawn me long before I ever started writing him.

"How could that be?" I whispered, to the savage, to myself.

He growled. He took some chicken feathers from his hair and put them into mine. He rubbed dirt from his hands across my face.

"Agh!" he said.

"Agh!" I answered. "Agh! Agh!"

He stamped the earth with his feet and I stamped the earth with mine. We grunted as we stamped and I knew how it felt to be the savage, to be truly wild.

I stared up at the family for the last time, then the savage threw the burning branch back towards the distant fire. It puttered and went out. We stood together in the darkness. He touched my brow just like he had touched Jess, and somehow I knew that my wounds would heal, that my sadness would start to fade, and I knew as well that somehow, in some weird way, everything that was happening was true. Everything. Even this next bit, this next amazing incredible bit, when the savage put his arm round me, and we listened together to the darkness, and I heard Dad's voice speaking to me. "Blue," he said. "Blue. Stay happy, son. I'm with you always." Then the voice was gone, and the savage was leading me back past the fire and the pictures, back towards the entrance. We stood there, two lads together, and we peered one more time into each other's eyes, then suddenly I was on the outside, at the ruined chapel, and I couldn't see the way back in again. But the chicken feathers were in my hair and the savage was in my heart and my dad was in my soul.

I held the feathers and I ran back home, and Mam

and Jess were in the house, grinning to see me, like always.

"Look at the state of this lad!" said Mam. She laughed. "And what are these?"

"They're feathers from the savage," I said, and we laughed and laughed.

Later, we had tea together and the darkness thickened in the town outside. I put the feathers in my hair and I remembered the smell and the touch of the savage in his cave, and I listened for Dad's voice. I smiled and growled softly and Jess giggled and Mam pointed at me.

"Look, Jess," she laughed. "Here's the savage, come to life in the real world."

# ELEVEN

It all seems ages back. We're still here in the house on Aidan's Lane. Jess is more grown up, of course. She's a proper little girl. She can read. She's still a great dancer. We tell her about Dad so it'll help her to remember. I suppose I'm more grown up as well, though some days I feel like a little kid inside. And my spelling's much improved, I'm pleased to say. We're not as sad as we were back then. In some weird way, the sadness helped us to get happy again. Hopper? He's quieter, not quite so stupid, not quite so horrible. I often catch him watching me. He never speaks, but I'm waiting for the day when he comes and asks me how I know about what happened to him in the night.

I went on writing "The Savage" till I'd written what happened in the cave on that last day. That was the story's end. Since then, I've kept it safe in a box under my bed. I've never told Mam about that day; about the pictures, about Dad's voice, about how the story and the real world came together. She's asked once or twice to read the whole thing, but I couldn't let her. It all seemed too complicated, too private, too weird. I've said, maybe one day, maybe one day. And being Mam, she says that's fine, and she's been content to wait.

But it's time to move forward, to share the story, to let it go.

I'm writing this right now, at the kitchen table. We've just had tea. It's dark outside. When I've finished this last bit, I'll pass it over to Mam along with the box with "The Savage" in it.

"This is for you, Mam," I'll say. "And for you, Jess. And for Dad."

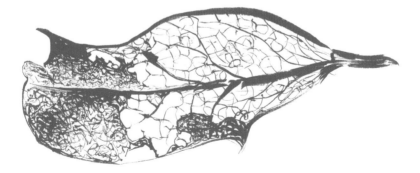

LEABHARLANN

UIMHIR ....................................................

RANG ....................................................

D h u . . . G a l l

## Acknowledgement:

*The Savage* was developed from
a short story commissioned by ITV and
Seven Stories: The Centre for Children's Books,
and produced by Planet North Productions.

This is a work of fiction. Names, characters, places and incidents are
either the product of the author's imagination or, if real, used fictitiously.

First published 2008 by Walker Books Ltd

87 Vauxhall Walk, London SE1 1 5HJ

2 4 6 8 10 9 7 5 3 1

Text © 2008 David Almond
Illustrations © 2008 Dave McKean

The right of David Almond and Dave McKean to be identified as author
and illustrator respectively of this work has been asserted by them in accordance
with the Copyright, Designs and Patents Act 1988

This book has been typeset in Gill Sans, Dink Scratch and Born Free

Printed in China

All rights reserved. No part of this book may be reproduced, transmitted or
stored in an information retrieval system in any form or by any means, graphic, electronic
or mechanical, including photocopying, taping and recording,
without prior written permission from the publisher.

British Library Cataloguing in Publication Data:
a catalogue record for this book is available
from the British Library

ISBN 978-1-4063-0815-0

www.walkerbooks.co.uk